HANSEL
and
GRETEL

RETOLD BY NADIA HIGGINS
ILLUSTRATED BY KATHLEEN PETELINSEK

Published by The Child's World®
1980 Lookout Drive • Mankato, MN 56003-1705
800-599-READ • www.childsworld.com

Acknowledgments
The Child's World®: Mary Berendes, Publishing Director
Red Line Editorial: Editorial direction
The Design Lab: Design, production, and illustration

ISBN 978-1623236090
LCCN 2013931328

Printed in the United States of America
Mankato, MN
July, 2013
PA02179

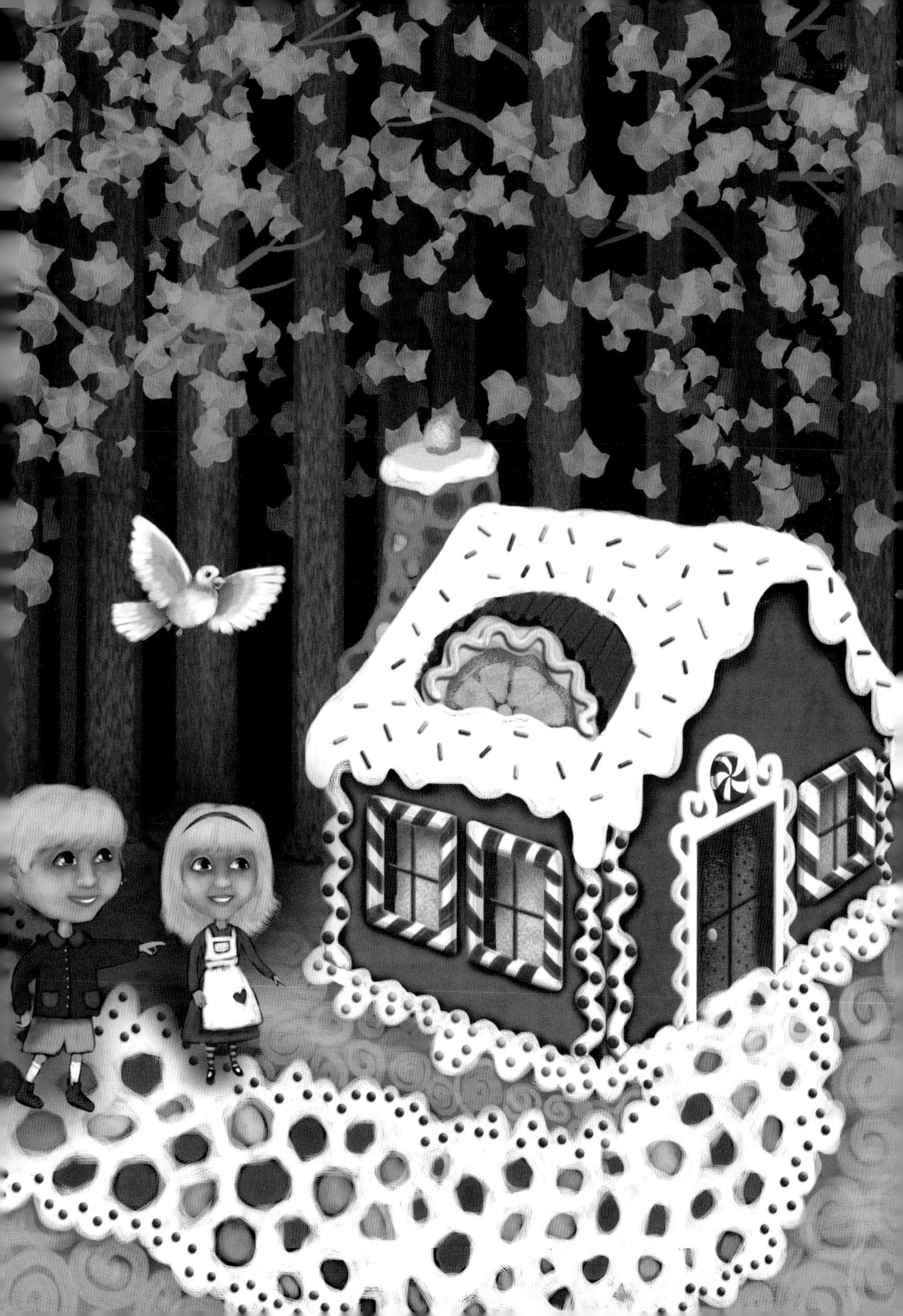

Long ago, a vast, mysterious forest stretched across the land. It held many wonders—and dangers, too. In these great woods lived a woodcutter with his two children and his new wife.

The family was facing a stretch of hard times. Food was scarce. The man's ribs showed along his back.

What was the poor woodcutter to do? His wife had an idea. "Those children are eating us out of house and home!" she said. "Tomorrow,

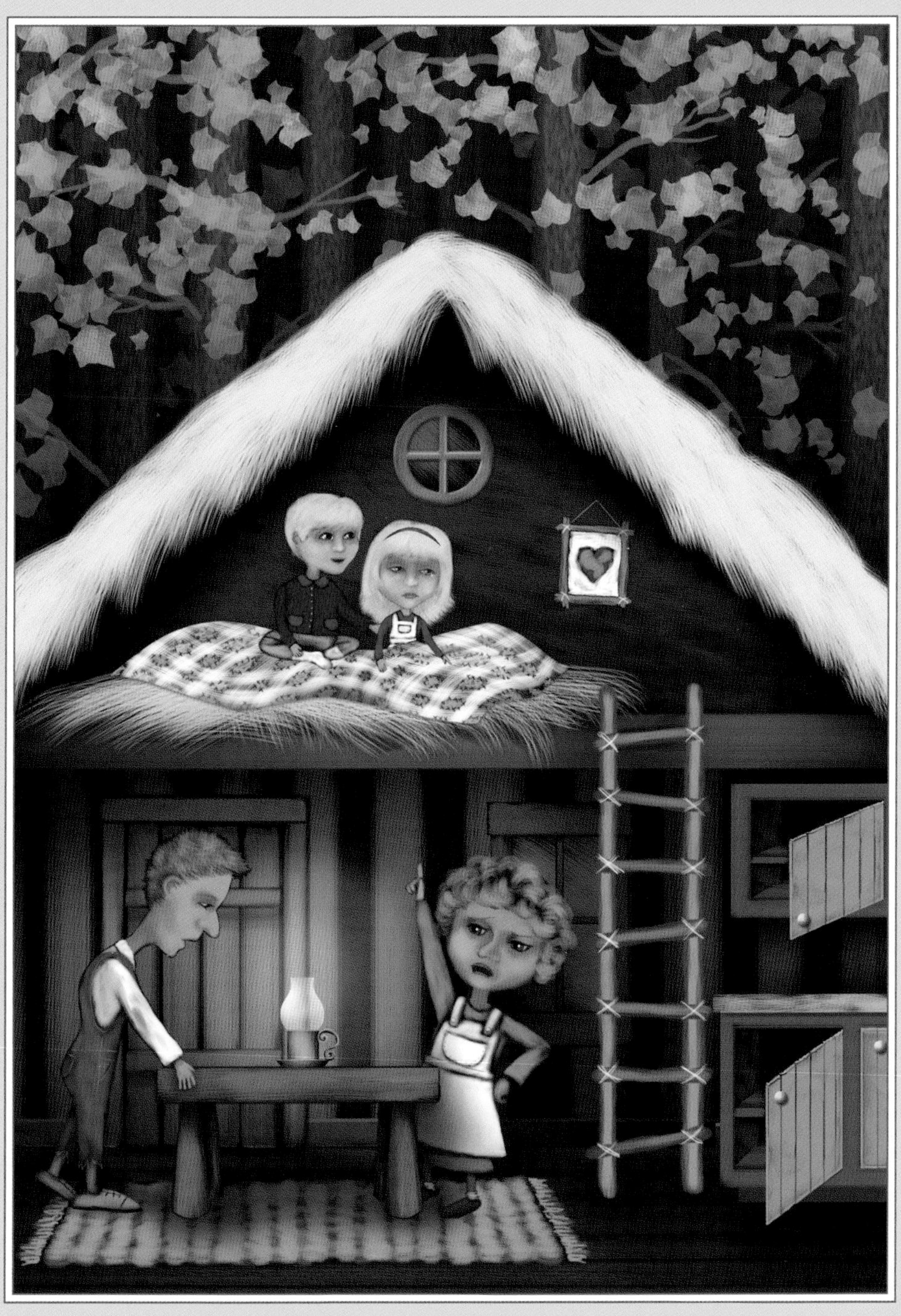

we'll take them deep into the forest and leave them there. They'll never find their way back."

"No!" The father's heart ached at the idea. But his stomach ached more. With great sadness, he gave in to his wife.

Now it so happened that the children had overheard every wicked word. The girl, Gretel, wept bitterly, as much from fear as from a broken heart.

"Don't cry," said her brother, Hansel.
"I will save us somehow."

The family set off for the forest early the
next morning to chop wood. Their stepmother
shoved a piece of bread into each child's hand.
"That's your lunch," she grunted.

This gave Hansel an idea. Little by little,
Hansel crumbled his bread and dropped the
crumbs along the trail as they walked.

After many hours, the family stopped. The woodcutter built a fire by a patch of moss. "Come, rest," he told his children, with great sorrow in his voice. "We are just going to go and chop some wood."

With that, Hansel and Gretel were left alone. When the sun began to set, it was clear they had been abandoned. Gretel looked to Hansel in despair. "Wait for the moon," Hansel reassured his sister. "It will show our trail of

crumbs back to the house." And so the weary children slept.

Sqweeeeee! Hansel and Gretel awoke to the sounds of screeching bats. A full moon had turned the trees into silvery ghosts. Stones shimmered on the forest floor. But not a single breadcrumb was to be seen.

"The birds have eaten them!" Gretel screamed. And she was right.

All the next day and night, the children wandered. They were so hungry, their legs began to shake. Finally, they collapsed under a tree and slept.

When they awoke, a white bird perched on the branch above them. It sang such sweet, tinkling notes. "Follow me," it seemed to say. And so the children did.

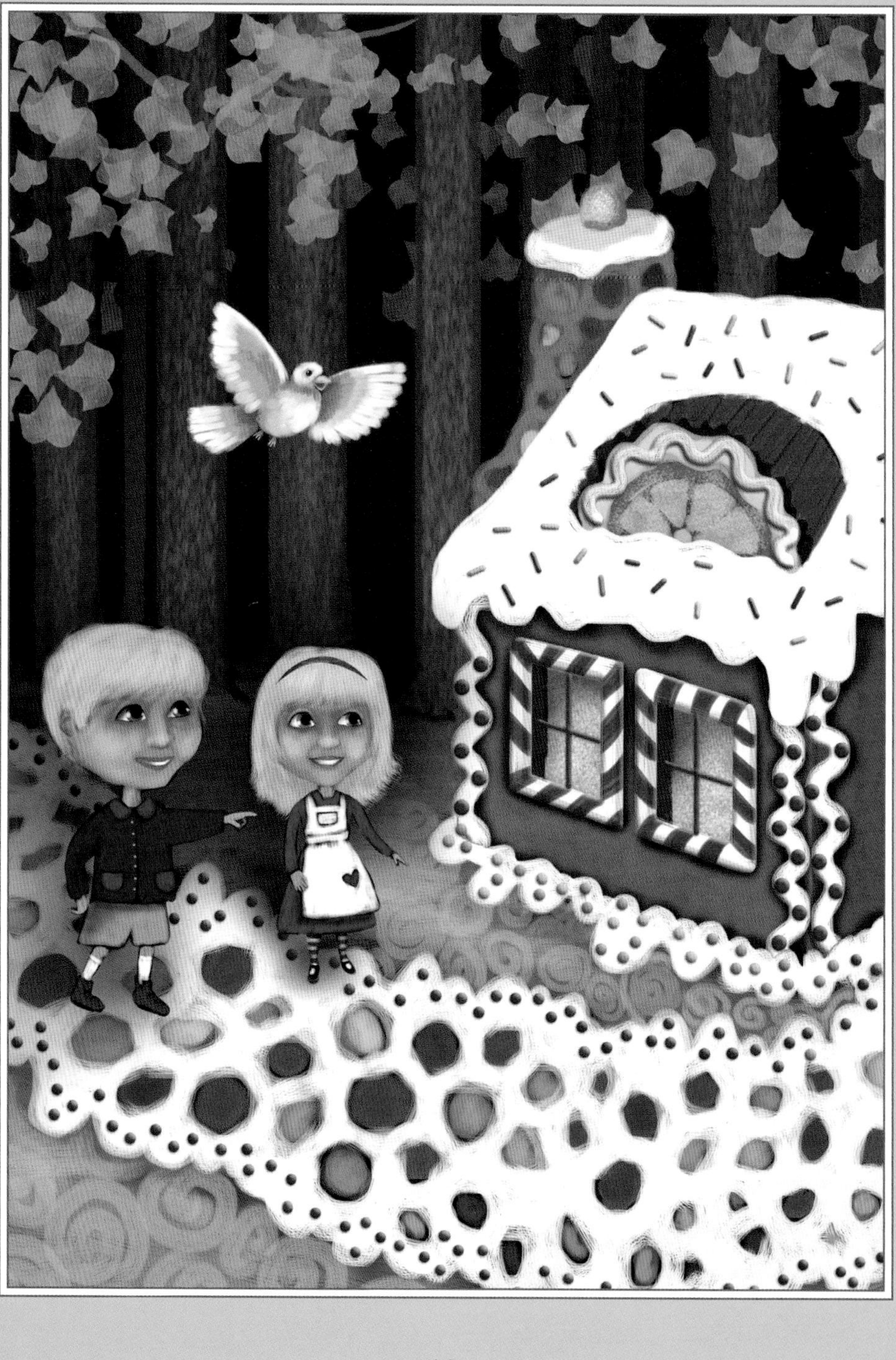

After a while, Gretel gasped, and Hansel yelled out, "Ha ha!" For they saw before them—could it be?—a house made of gingerbread, with cake for a roof and windows glittering with sugar!

The two hungry children attacked that house. Hansel was devouring a chunk of roof and Gretel was licking a shard of window when an old hunched woman emerged from the house.

"Oh, you poor dears," she said, smiling into the children's frightened faces. "Come, be my guests." She led them inside to a table covered with mouth-watering treats.

Did the children see danger in the woman's red eyes? Of course. But they ignored it because they were so hungry. And how they feasted! Afterward, they squirmed happily into thick feather beds.

The woman chuckled as she gazed upon their sleeping faces. "What a tasty treat they will make for my birthday," she crooned.

For the old woman was really a witch. She used her house to lure children, whom she ate!

The next morning, the witch grabbed Hansel from his bed. The boy kicked and punched. But he could not free himself, for the witch had incredible strength. She threw Hansel into a cage and locked the door.

"Go fetch your brother something to eat," the witch then snarled at Gretel. "He needs some fattening up!"

Day after day, poor Gretel brought her brother platters of fried potatoes and chicken, mountains of ham, and tall cakes oozing with icing. Meanwhile, the witch offered Gretel only scraps, but it hardly mattered. Her brother shared his food with her right beneath the witch's nose. As with all witches, her red eyes could barely see.

Each morning, the witch commanded that Hansel stick out his finger so she could feel how fat he'd grown. And each morning, Hansel stuck out a chicken bone instead. Why Hansel stayed so thin, the witch could not guess.

Finally, the witch's birthday came. "I'm eating that boy, fat or thin," she proclaimed. "Prepare the oven, Gretel!"

Gretel did the witch's bidding with trembling hands. When the fire was crackling hot, the witch smiled sweetly at her. "My dear, won't you crawl inside the oven and see that the fire is properly made?"

Well, Gretel guessed what the witch was up to! The wicked creature was going to slam the door and make the girl an appetizer before the

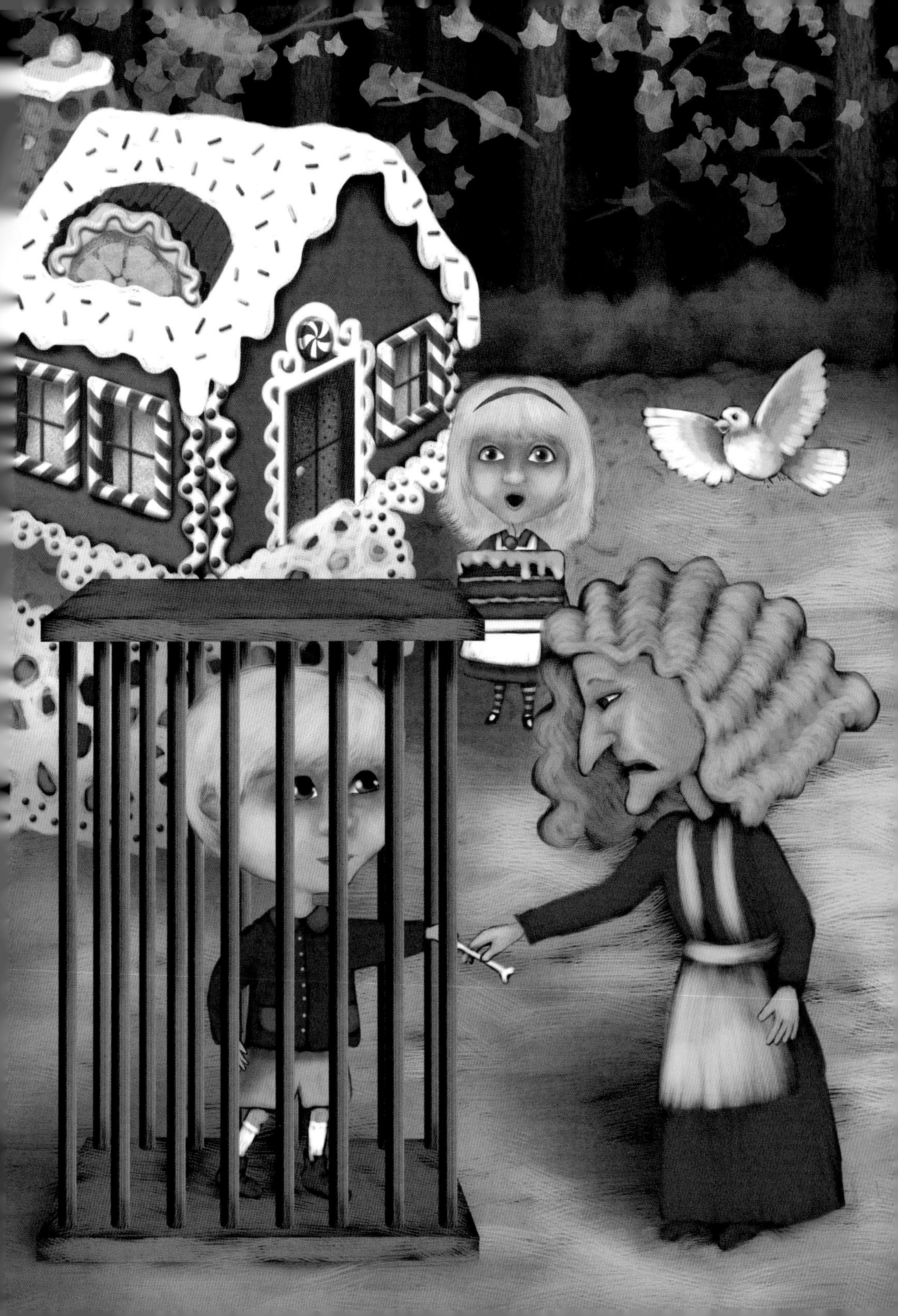

meal of her brother. Gretel quickly thought of a plan.

"Oh, but silly me, I don't know how," Gretel replied with wide eyes.

"Stupid girl!" the witch snapped. "It's easy. See?" The witch climbed onto the oven's ledge and leaned her head toward the dancing flames.

Gretel seized her chance. She shoved the witch into the oven and slammed the door.

The witch howled horribly as she burned in her own trap. Gretel covered her ears and ran to free her brother.

How the children rejoiced! They held hands and danced around the yard. "We're free, free, free!" they sang. And what was that?

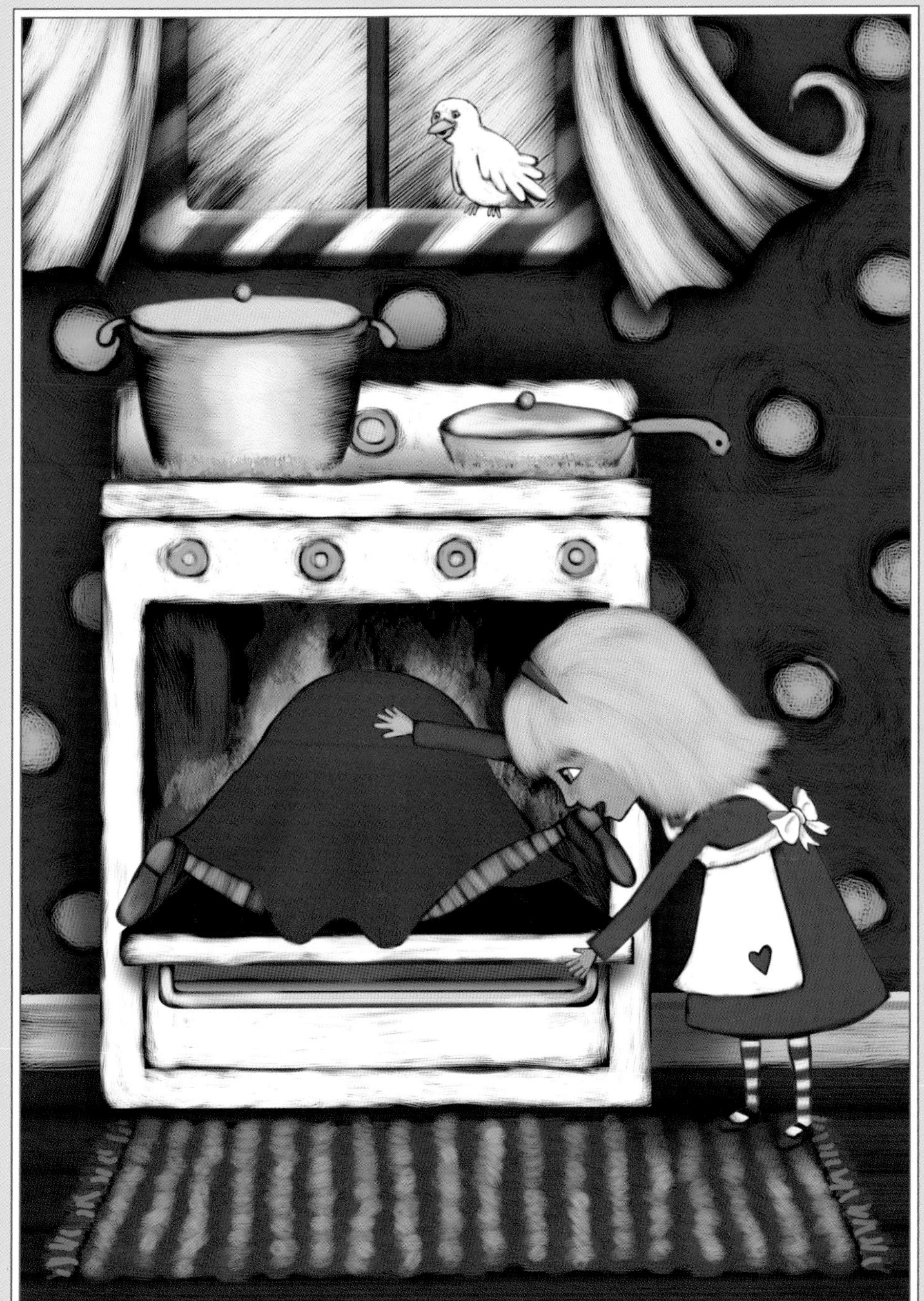

They heard a cheery, tinkling sound above their heads. The white bird was celebrating with them!

The children were anxious to find their way home. But first, they reentered the witch's house. Why? Because while feasting that first night, Hansel and Gretel had laid their eyes upon more than just a table of food.

The witch had heaps of trunks stacked in every corner of the cottage, and each trunk

was filled with jewels. The children flung the trunks open. Dazzling gems and pearls sparkled before them. Hansel filled his pockets, and Gretel filled her apron pockets.

When the children had all the jewels they could carry, they set off through the woods, with the white bird leading the way. The bird called to them with her special song. They followed her across a meadow and around a pond.

Soon, Hansel and Gretel began to recognize the path. There was the oak they loved to climb! And strawberry plants they picked in summer! And, oh, their father running toward them with open arms!

The grief-stricken man had regretted leaving his children and had been searching

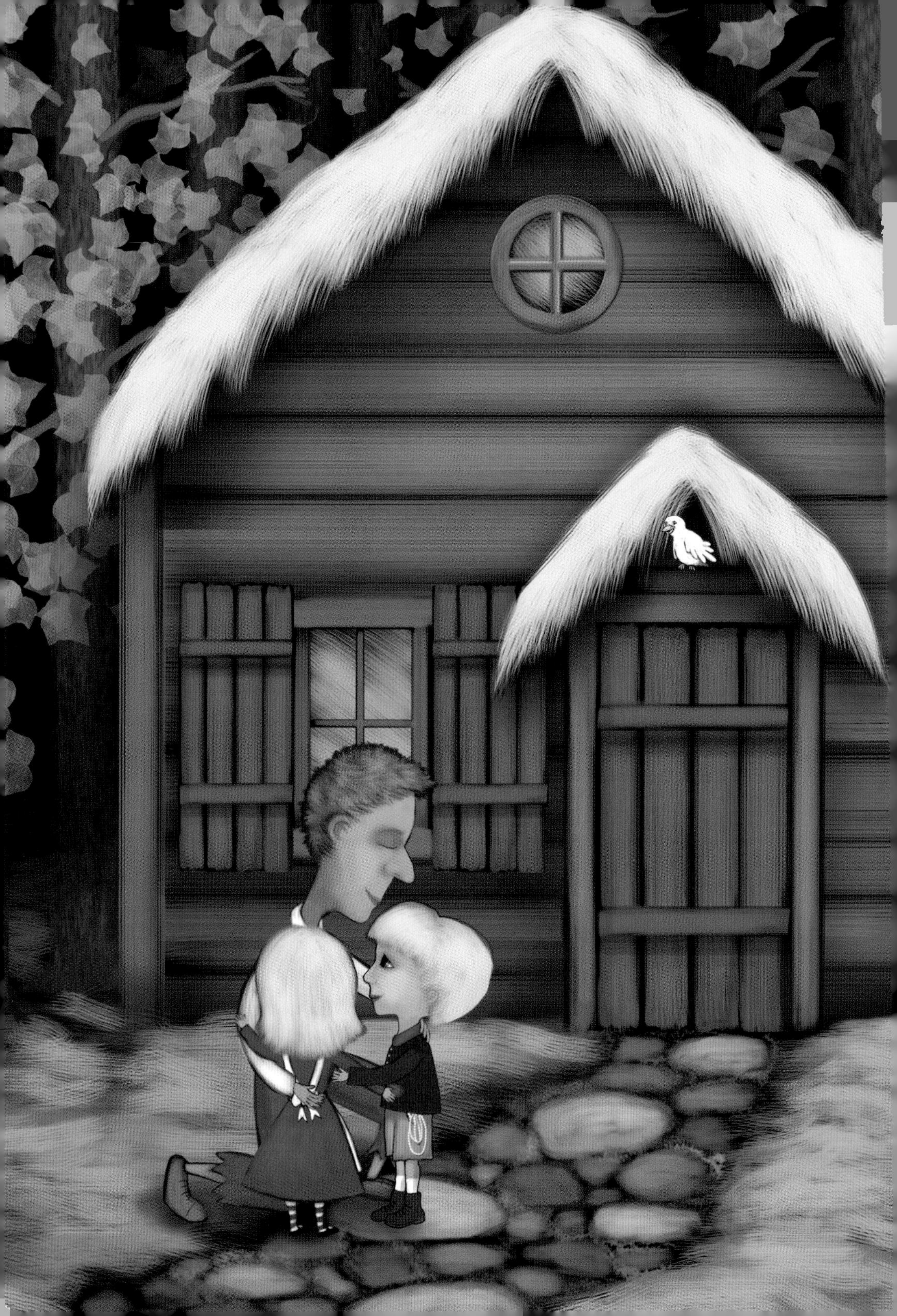

for them ever since. Tears streamed down his face as he hugged and kissed them. "My treasures!" he cried.

Hansel and Gretel giggled as they poured a shower of jewels from their pockets. With so much wealth, the family would never starve again.

As for the wicked stepmother? She died from an unknown cause while the children were away. The family never mentioned her again.

Fairy Tales

Hansel and Gretel's story was first written down and published in 1812 by Jacob and Wilhelm Grimm of Germany, better known as the Brothers Grimm. However, the Brothers Grimm didn't invent the story. It had been told for hundreds of years. The story may have originated in the 1300s, when a great famine spread across Europe. During this time, parents struggled to keep their families from starving.

The Brothers Grimm enjoyed all types of tales. They traveled far, to small villages and distant farmhouses, to collect stories. Sometimes, they simply wrote down what they were told. More often, they combined different versions of stories, including their favorite parts from various sources.

Why are we still reading about Hansel and Gretel today? After all, the story has its share of plot holes. Why does the witch bother fattening up Hansel, but not Gretel? How does Gretel so easily release Hansel from his cage? And why didn't she do so earlier, since the witch couldn't see anyway?

Maybe this story isn't about making sense. The story touches something more mysterious inside of us. Have you ever walked through deep, dark woods? It can feel magical, and a little scary. And who hasn't had a heart-stopping moment when they've lost sight of their parents in public? Hansel and Gretel's story adds a "what if?" to this common fear. What if your parents really were gone—and on purpose? No doubt, you would want to be as clever and brave as Hansel and Gretel!

ABOUT THE AUTHOR

Nadia Higgins is the author of more than sixty books for children. She lives in Minneapolis, Minnesota, with her husband and two daughters.

ABOUT THE ILLUSTRATOR

Kathleen Petelinsek loves to draw and paint. She lives next to a lake in southern Minnesota with her husband, Dale; two daughters, Leah and Anna; two dogs, Gary and Rex; and her fluffy cat, Emma.